HEL

I'm *Geronimo Sutton*'s sister. As I'm sure you know from my brother's bestselling novels, I'm a special correspondent for *The Rodent's Gazette*, Mouse Island's most famous newspaper. Unlike my 'fraidy mouse brother, I absolutely adore traveling, having adventures, and meeting rodents from all around the world!

The adventure I want to tell you about begins at Mouseford Academy, the school I went to when I was a young mouseling. I had such a great experience there as a student that I came back to teach a journalism class.

When I returned as a grown mouse, I met five really special students: Colette, Nicky, Pamela, Paulina, and Violet. You could hardly imagine five more different mouselings, but they became great friends right away. And they liked me so much that they decided to name their group after me: the Thea Sisters! I was so touched by that, I decided to write about their adventures. So turn the page to read a fabumouse adventure about the

THEA SISTERS!

Name: Nicky

Nickname: Nic

Home: Australia

Secret ambition: Wants to be an ecologist.

Loves: Open spaces and nature.

Strengths: She is always in a good mood, as long as she's outdoors!

Weaknesses: She can't sit still!

Secret: Nicky is claustrophobic—she can't stand being in small, tight places.

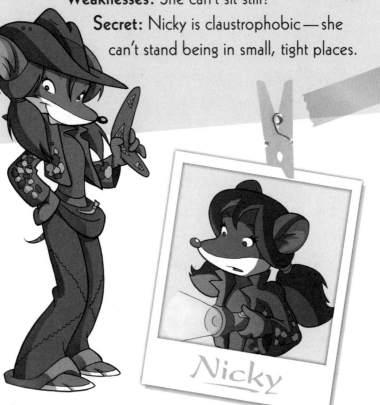

Nicky

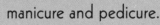

COLETTE

Name: Colette

Nickname: It's Colette, please. (She can't stand nicknames.)

Home: France

Secret ambition: Colette is very particular about her appearance. She wants to be a fashion writer.

Loves: The color pink.

Strengths: She's energetic and full of great ideas.

Weaknesses: She's always late!

Secret: To relax, there's nothing Colette likes more than a manicure and pedicure.

Colette

VIOLET

Name: Violet
Nickname: Vi
Home: China
Secret ambition: Wants to become a great violinist.
Loves: Books! She is a real intellectual, just like my brother, Geronimo.
Strengths: She's detail-oriented and always open to new things.
Weaknesses: She is a bit sensitive and can't stand being teased. And if she doesn't get enough sleep, she can be a real grouch!
Secret: She likes to unwind by listening to classical music and drinking green tea.

Violet

Name: Paulina

Nickname: Polly

Home: Peru

Secret ambition: Wants to be a scientist.

Loves: Traveling and meeting people from all over the world. She is also very close to her sister, Maria.

Strengths: Loves helping other rodents.

Weaknesses: She's shy and can be a bit clumsy.

Secret: She is a computer genius!

PAULINA

PAULINA

Name: Pamela
Nickname: Pam
Home: Tanzania

PAMELA

Secret ambition: Wants to become a sports journalist or a car mechanic.

Loves: Pizza, pizza, and more pizza! She'd eat pizza for breakfast if she could.

Strengths: She is a peacemaker. She can't stand arguments.

Weaknesses: She is very impulsive.

Secret: Give her a screwdriver and any mechanical problem will be solved!

Pamela

Geronimo Stilton

Thea Stilton
BIG TROUBLE IN THE BIG APPLE

Scholastic Inc.

New York   Toronto   London   Auckland

Sydney   Mexico City   New Delhi   Hong Kong

No part of this book may be reproduced, stored in a retrieval system, or transmitted in any form or by any means, electronic, mechanical, photocopying, recording, or otherwise, without written permission from the copyright holder. For information regarding permission, please contact: Atlantyca S.p.A., Via Leopardi 8, 20123 Milan, Italy; e-mail foreignrights@atlantyca.it, www.atlantyca.com.

ISBN 978-0-545-22775-9

www.geronimostilton.com

Published by Scholastic Inc., 557 Broadway, New York, NY 10012. SCHOLASTIC and associated logos are trademarks and/or registered trademarks of Scholastic Inc.

Stilton is the name of a famous English cheese. It is a registered trademark of the Stilton Cheese Makers' Association. For more information, go to www.stiltoncheese.com.

Text by Thea Stilton
Original title *Grosso guaio a New York*
Cover by Effeeffestudios
Illustrations by Alessandro Battan, Jacopo Brandi, Monica Catalano, Carlo Alberto Fiaschi, Michela Frare, Daniela Geremia, Sonia Matrone, Elisabetta Melaranci, Marco Meloni, Roberta Pierpaoli, Arianna Rea, Maurizio Roggerone, Raffaella Seccia, and Roberta Tedeschi
Color by Tania Boccalini, Alessandra Bracaglia, Connie Daidone, Ketty Formaggio, Daniela Geremia, Nicola Pasquetto, Elena Sanjust, and Micaela Tangorra
Graphics by Paola Cantoni

Special thanks to Kathryn Cristaldi
Translated by Emily Clement
Interior design by Kay Petronio

12   15 16/0

Printed in the U.S.A.   40
First printing, September 2011

ON THE WAY TO WHALE ISLAND

It was a gorgeous fall morning in New Mouse City when I boarded a ferry headed straight for **Whale Island**. I was so excited, my fur *tingled*. I was making a visit to my old school, **MOUSEFORD ACADEMY**.

Oh, excuse me. I forgot to introduce myself. I'm **THEA STILTON**, a special correspondent for *The Rodent's Gazette*, the most famouse *NEWSPAPER* on Mouse Island.

Professor **Octavius de Mousus** had invited me for some sort of special event. (He was being very secretive about it.)

So I asked my brother, Geronimo, if he needed me for the newspaper, and he said I was free to go. You know Geronimo, right? He's the head of *The Rodent's Gazette,* and technically my boss.

I said good-bye to everyone at the office, packed my suitcase in record time, and **SAILED** off from New Mouse City in a **ferry** to Mouseford. Yes, **CAPTAIN** vince Guymouse's ferry is still the **ONly** way to travel to Whale Island, where Mouseford is located.

"We'll be there so *FAST* your fur will fly, Miss Stilton!" Vince **PROMISED** when I told him I was in a hurry. But a few minutes later, Vince slowed to a crawl. I was **FLABBERGASTED**.

I marched into the pilot's cabin. "What are you **DOING**?" I squeaked. "At this rate my fur will be **WHITE** by the time we reach Whale Island!"

Vince pointed to a nearby cruise ship. A group of pretty female mice were sunbathing on the deck. "I was just being friendly," he said, waving desperately at the sunbathers. They ignored him.

I glared at Vince.

Then I **WRENCHED** the controls from his paws, increased the speed of the engine, and took off. **VROOOOOOOOM!**

Whale Island appeared on the horizon.

I laughed. "If you want something done right, sometimes you have to **do it yourself**!"

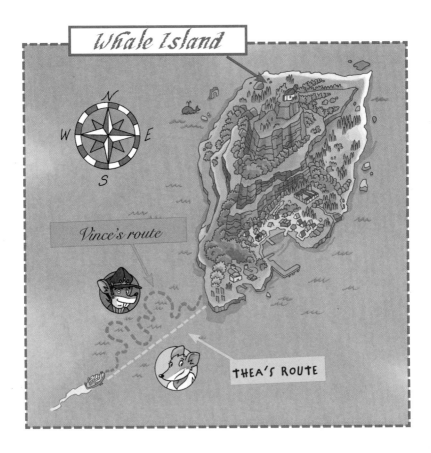

HURRY, THEA!

I arrived at **MOUSEFORD ACADEMY** right on time.

Of course, I wasn't really sure what I was on time for, but I couldn't wait to find out! Unlike my boring older brother, Geronimo, I love surprises!

I was hoping my dear friends the THEA SISTERS—*Nicky*, PAULINA, **Violet**, PAMELA, and *Colette*—might meet me, but they didn't. Instead, the professor was waiting for me at the academy's entrance.

"Hurry, THEA! The MARATHON has started!" he squeaked.

MARATHON?!

The students and teachers had gathered in the school's lounge. They were watching the **Big Apple Marathon** on TV.

WHAT A WELCOME!

As soon as I entered the room, I realized everyone was STARING at me intensely, waving banners, caps, and flags in the air.

What a welcome!

I must say, even though it was a little embarrassing, I was truly honored by their obvious affection for me. Many students were **CHEERING** and shouting.

"Thank you all so much," I said with a beaming smile. "You didn't have to do all this for me!"

"But, um, THEA . . . ," the professor whispered in my ear. "They're not cheering for you. They're trying to get you to move. You're standing in front of the television screen."

Oops. I hadn't realized that behind me there was a giant television screen, which was showing the **MARATHON**. Feeling embarrassed, I sat down on a nearby chair and looked at the screen. I could hardly believe it when I spotted one of the THEA SISTERS in the middle of the crowd of runners!

"NICKY!" I shouted.

NICKY   Ratridge runner

"Do you like the surprise?" the professor asked, winking at me. "Nicky is competing on behalf of **MOUSEFORD**. She's there with the other THEA SISTERS. Paulina is sending us this video from her computer."

I grabbed a flag and started to shout at the top of my lungs, "Come on, Nicky! Go, Mouseford!"

But while I was cheering, I noticed that Nicky looked exhausted, and that her eyes were FIXED on another athlete in front of her. The mouse was wearing a jersey with a coat of arms I knew well: a blue snake wrapped around the letter **R** on a silver background. It was the crest of **RATRIDGE ACADEMY**, Mouseford's biggest rival.

At that moment, I realized I had just discovered a **fabumouse** subject for my next book. It started something like this. . . .

THE CHALLENGE

It was fall, and a new school year was beginning at Mouseford. Friends greeted each other with **HUGS** and compared schedules to see if they had signed up for any of the same classes.

Like the other students, the Thea Sisters were full of *ENERGY*.

But Nicky was probably the most **ENERGETIC** of the bunch.

That was because this year she had decided to make one of her greatest dreams come true. She was going to run in the Big Apple Marathon in **NEW YORK**!

Every day, she woke up at dawn to train, running along the **STREETS** and to the island's beaches.

Nicky ran for miles and miles **up** and

... uphill ...

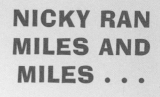

... and down ...

... all the way to the ocean's edge on the beach.

The other Thea Sisters supported her in every way!

DOWN the hills of Whale Island. Some days the sunshine would **WARM** her whiskers, making her smile. And other days the rain would **soak** her fur so badly she looked like a drowned rat when she finished!

Training for a race is always hard work. But training for a marathon is **EXTRA**-hard work, because it is such a **looooong** race!

Of course, the Thea Sisters encouraged Nicky every pawstep of the way. They made sure she drank enough fluids and ate healthy meals. They made sure she remembered to **stretch** and got plenty of rest.

Nicky was thrilled that her friends were so proud of her. But she had no idea she had another faithful supporter.

One day, *Professor* Octavius de Mousus called all five of the THEA SISTERS into his office.

"What do you think he wants?" wondered Violet.

"Maybe he needs me to fix a **FLAT** tire on his car," guessed Pamela.

"Maybe he wants me to update his *look*. You know I love fashion," said Colette.

"Or maybe he found out I'm practicing for the marathon and wants to tell me I can't go!" worried Nicky.

When the girls stepped into the professor's office, he began squeaking in a solemn tone.

"I've learned that Nicky is preparing for the **Big Apple Marathon**," he said.

Everyone gulped.

"I've also learned that our rival, Ratridge Academy, has entered a student named **Rhonda Razorpaws**," he continued. "She's fast, but I think our Nicky is even

faster. I would be **proud** if you would represent Mouseford Academy, Nicky."

And with that, the professor took from a drawer a beautiful sports jersey with the academy's crest.

What a **fabumouse** gift!

Nicky felt full of pride and energy.

"It will be an honor to wear it!" she responded, deeply moved.

"Go, Mouseford, and go, Nicky!"

the Thea Sisters shouted all together.

"And as for you four," the professor added, turning to Paulina, Pamela, Violet, and Colette, "since I know you will be a great SUPPORT to your friend, I am giving you permission to join her in the BiG APPLE. I hope you all have a cheesy good time!"

NEW YORK, HERE WE COME!

Finally, the day of the big trip arrived. Pamela, Violet, Paulina, and Nicky packed their bags in a *FLASH*. But Colette took forever trying to SQUEEZE all her favorite outfits into one suitcase.

VINCE FLO SAM BELLA

PAM

GEORGIE

"How do you girls do it?" she marveled.

The **THEA SISTERS** had agreed to take only one bag each, since they would all be staying at Pamela's family's house.

"Forget our BAGS, how will they find enough room for US?" Violet had asked. "Don't you have twelve rodents in your family, Pamela?"

PAMELA'S FAMILY

SPIKE

JO

PAPA JOHNNY

GRANDPA ALBIE

PEGGY

GUS

MAMA GIANNA

"**Thirteen** including Grandpa Albie!" Pam squeaked, *smiling*. "He just moved to New York from Tanzania a few years ago. That's where my mom's family is from. But you haven't seen my house yet. It belonged to **Frankie Tortellini**. He had **EIGHTEEN** children!"

Frankie Tortellini

Dad, when he was young

"And who was this guy with so many children?" Colette asked.

"He was my dad's **BOSS**," replied Pamela. "He was the one who taught him all the secrets of a genuine Neapolitan pizza! When he decided to return to Italy, he sold the house and the shop to my dad. And now my parents have put all their savings into redoing the **Pizzeria**. By now they must have finished working on it . . . and I can't wait to see how it looks!"

Pamela hugged her **BEST FRIENDS**.

"I'm so happy you're coming to the **BiG APPLE**!" she squeaked excitedly.

Colette **BLINKED**. "What?! You mean your house is shaped like a big apple?" she asked.

"No, silly. The **BiG APPLE** is the nickname for New York City!" Paulina giggled.

Now it was Colette's turn to laugh. "So that's why they call it the **Big Apple Marathon**. I thought maybe they gave out apples after the race," she chuckled.

Still laughing, the Thea Sisters grabbed their bags and headed for the dock where the ferry for Mouse Island was waiting. A huge banner greeted them. It read *Bon voyage!* The members of the academy's **ATHLETIC CLUB** stood below the banner, waving.

"Good luck, Nicky!" they yelled as the ferry sailed away.

As the Mouseford Academy flag grew SMALLER and SMALLER behind them, the THEA SISTERS turned their attention forward.

"New York, here we come!" shouted Pamela.

RHONDA RAZORPAWS

The New Mouse City Airport was a **WHIRL** of activity. Rodents scampered here and there, greeting loved ones, buying gifts at the airport shops, and munching on fast food. Nicky's head was spinning. Just then a **TALL** mouseling with **long** legs zipped by. She was dressed in a **RATRIDGE ACADEMY** tracksuit.

"That must be **Rhonda Razorpaws**, the athlete from Ratridge!" Nicky squeaked. "Maybe we can go for a **RUN** together before the marathon!" But when Nicky introduced herself to Rhonda, the other mouse just **SNEERED**.

"**GOOD LUCK** making it to the finish line, Nicky," she snorted.

Then Rhonda joined a tall rodent with

a **MUStacHe**. He was carrying an **ENORMOUSE** load of luggage and motioning for Rhonda to **hurry**.

"And that must be Karl Razorpaws, her father," Nicky said.

"He was a **RUGBY** champion years ago. Now he's her coach, and he's very strict."

Violet winked. "If he taught her to run as well as he taught her good manners, then you're already pawsteps ahead of her, my dear Nicky!"

NEW YORK!
NEW YORK!

The five FRiENDS landed in **NEW YORK** while it was still afternoon. Unfortunately, when they arrived, New York was covered in CLOUDS. Pamela pouted, as if the city were doing it just to **SPiTE** her. She had wanted the city to look beautiful for her friends.

But Nicky was thrilled. "It's a good thing it's not SUNNY! I hope that the sky stays cloudy until the marathon," she squeaked. "There's nothing more exhausting than running **TWENTY-SiX MiLES** in the roasting sunshine!"

Pamela grinned. Nicky was right. Plus, even on a cloudy day, New York City made her whiskers tingle. She led her friends through a maze of escalators and hallways to the airport exit, where her brother Vince would be waiting for them.

But when they arrived, Vince was nowhere in sight.

"How could Vince be late today OF ALL DAYS?!" Pamela complained in frustration.

Paulina was fascinated by all the rodents racing past. They were from all over the world! She noticed a mouse clutching a sign in his paws. It read THEA SISTERS.

"That's us!" the mouselings cried, running up to the mouse.

"Hey there!" the mouse said. "My name's SAMMY P. ZIPMEISTER, but you can just call me ZIPPER. I'm your ride to your destination, which I'm told is TRIBECA."

He turned to Pamela and grabbed her suitcase. "You're Pam, right?" he guessed.

Before Pam could answer, **ZIPPER** took off like a *shot*. The Thea Sisters *raced* after him.

They followed him to a bright **yellow** taxicab and climbed inside. "We'll take a nice **scenic** route, OK?" he suggested without waiting for a response.

They hadn't even settled themselves on the seats before the taxi took off like a **ROCKET**, darting between cars through the city **STREETS**.

The **THEA SISTERS** cried out in surprise. The only one who didn't even blink was Pamela, who sat *calmly* behind Zipper.

TAXI

New York City taxis are called yellow cabs because of their distinctive color. The first taxis were painted red and green but then were repainted yellow so they could be more easily identified as licensed vehicles. Today there are more than 13,000 taxis operating in New York City.

The other mice **CLUNG** to their seats for dear life as the city sights **WHIZZED** by outside their windows. They were almost too afraid to look!

"It sure is getting **cold** out," Zipper remarked. "The wind is blowing from the north. Do you see how the clouds are moving?"

Pam raised her eyes to the sky, and a beautiful **PINK** and **ORANGE** sunset appeared on the horizon. As the taxi turned onto the Brooklyn Bridge, the **NEW YORK CITY SKYLINE**, with its famous stretch of skyscrapers, appeared before the Thea Sisters.

ZIPPER slowed down so they could enjoy the view.

"Look, everyone!" Pamela sighed. "Isn't the city *beautiful?*"

"**WOW!**" Nicky squeaked.

"**WOW!**" Paulina, Violet, and Colette echoed.

Pamela grinned. How could anyone not fall in love with New York City?

WHAT A
WELCOME!

When the **THEA SISTERS** arrived in the **TRIBECA** neighborhood, the **sun** had almost set.

They didn't even have time to say goodbye to **ZIPPER** before the taxi took off again with a *squeal* of the tires.

SKREEEEEEEEEEEECH!

"Sorry I can't hang!" he shouted, **waving**

TRIBECA

This neighborhood's name comes from the phrase **TRI**angle **BE**low **CA**nal Street, because of its triangular shape. Not too long ago, Tribeca was home to small factories and warehouses. Now it's a fashionable residential neighborhood, frequented by celebrities.

his paw out the window. "Got to keep **MOVING**! Catch you later!"

"Byeeeeee!" the mouselings called out as they waved back.

Just then the door to Pamela's apartment building **SWUNG** open.

"PAMELA!!!" voices squeaked.

The THEA SISTERS were whisked into a redbrick, three-story building. They soon found themselves in a large room that was decorated with **COLORFUL** banners and balloons.

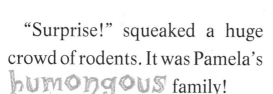

"Surprise!" squeaked a huge crowd of rodents. It was Pamela's humongous family!

The twins, Peggy and Gus, proudly presented their sister with a crayon drawing they had made for her.

SMACK! SMACK! SMACK! SMACK!

Pam covered them in kisses. Then she introduced the rest of her family to her friends. "This is my dad, Papa Johnny, but everyone calls him PJ. And this is my mom, Mama Gianna, and my dear grandpa Albie," she said with a smile.

All nine brothers and sisters were there in a happy jumble: Gus, Peggy, Vince, Sam, Georgie, Flo, Jo, Spike, and Bella.

Everyone hugged and *kissed*. When

they were done, they hugged and kissed some more!

Then they asked Nicky a million QUESTIONS about the marathon.

The Thea Sisters could hardly believe it. In just a few minutes, they felt like part of the **family**!

"My house is your house!" Papa Johnny said. "If you need anything, help yourself!"

SPIKE

MAMMA GIANNA

PAPA JOHNNY

FLO

GUS

PEGGY

There was a low **GRUMBLE**.

"Actually, there *is* something we need, Dad . . . ," Pamela said softly, patting her stomach.

"Yes?" asked her dad, looking concerned. "When are we going to eat?! We're starving!"

Papa Johnny laughed. "Of course!" he squeaked. "Everyone to the Pizzeria!"

TRÈS CHIC!

They didn't have to go very far: The pizzeria was located on the ground floor of the building.

As soon as they entered, a feeling of **warmth** surrounded them. The walls were a beautiful shade of **aquamarine**, and the tables were set with **blue** tablecloths. Delicate candleholders made of blown glass and a vase of fresh *flowers* decorated each table.

"**Très chic!**" Colette commented. "How elegant!"

"What do you think, Pamela?" Vince asked. It was clear he valued his sister's opinion.

"It's **fabumouse!**" Pam replied, impressed.

While Vince showed the pizzeria to

Pamela, the rest of the family started to **cook**. Mama Gianna and Georgie prepared the toppings for the pizza while Flo and Jo finished arranging the tables.

Paulina watched Sam and Spike as they **prepared** the dough.

First they **FLATTENED** the dough on the counter until it formed a disk. Then they *spun* it above their heads, throwing it into the air in a thousand *twists* and **turns**.

What an **amazing** sight! They worked just like jugglers in a circus!

Pamela grabbed a ball of dough from a tray and started to pound it into shape. "Watch this!" she exclaimed, eager to show her friends her own pizza-making skills. A minute later she tossed the pizza dough into the air, where it **spun** above her head once, twice, three times. . . .

Then it landed—**splat**—right on Colette's head!

"It's okay, it's okay, it's okay . . . ," Colette chanted to herself, picking the **sticky** dough out of her fur. She didn't want to make a scene in front of Pamela's family, but it took all her strength to keep from **screaming**!

"Maybe I've lost my touch," Pamela admitted.

"Maybe just a little bit," Violet replied, smiling and Winking at her friends.

Just then an inviting aroma filled the air. The pizzas had come out of the oven.

"Dinner's ready!" Bella shouted.

Vince and PJ pushed the tables close together to form one **long** table. For the occasion, Pam's dad had created a SPECIAL pizza just for the Thea Sisters. He'd made it in the shape of a giant heart and covered it with lots of whisker-licking-good toppings, including cheesy mozzarella, yellow peppers, pepperoni, spicy jalapeño, shrimp, and tasty mushrooms.

It was an incredibly amazing pizza!

A NIGHT IN MANHATTAN

After dinner, Pam suggested the Thea Sisters take a walk in **Manhattan**. Actually, Pamela had a specific destination in mind. So the group left the bright **LIGHTS** of West Broadway and the **SPARKLING** lights of Greenwich Street and headed for the piers.

The piers stretched out like long, dark fingers on the water of the **HUDSON RIVER**.

The **THEA SISTERS** walked along a sidewalk that ended when it came to a **WOODEN** dock. Under the dock, the dark water of the river flowed.

And from the dark water of the bay in the **distance** rose the Statue of Liberty, shining like a **STAR**!

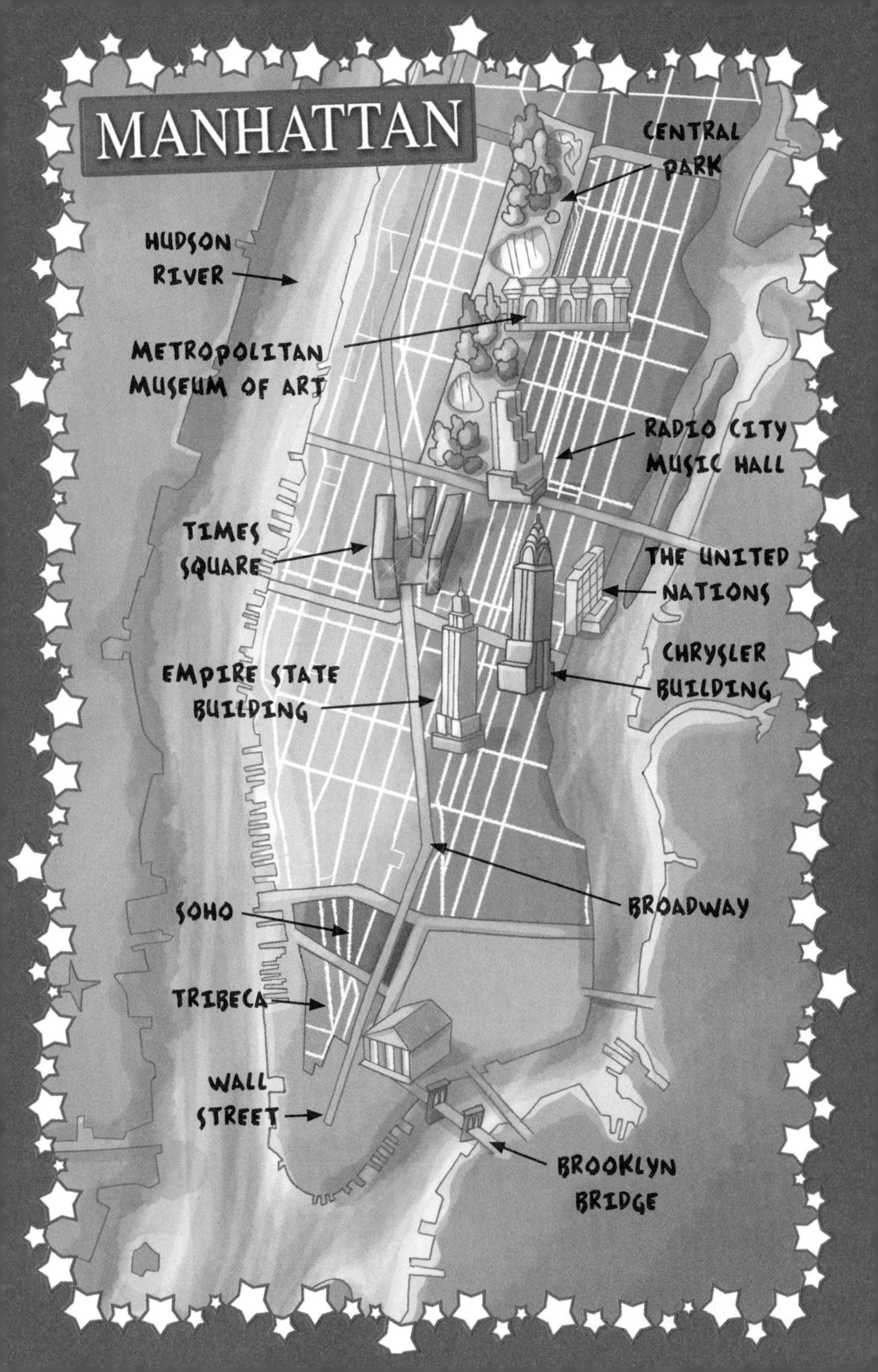

MANHATTAN

CENTRAL PARK

HUDSON RIVER

METROPOLITAN MUSEUM OF ART

RADIO CITY MUSIC HALL

TIMES SQUARE

THE UNITED NATIONS

EMPIRE STATE BUILDING

CHRYSLER BUILDING

SOHO

BROADWAY

TRIBECA

WALL STREET

BROOKLYN BRIDGE

"This is the place I love most in all of New York! I guess you could say it's my special spot," Pamela squeaked, hoping her friends would agree. "What do you think? Isn't it **AMAZING**?"

"It's unbelievable!" Paulina exclaimed as Nicky, Violet, and Colette squeezed in to give Pam a furry group **hug**.

Across the water, the statue's torch twinkled in the night sky.

WHO IS PHOENIX?

"We'd better head back," Pam said after a while.

"Yes, it's getting late," Paulina agreed.

But as the five friends turned to head home, they noticed a **DARK** figure dragging a cart with small **wheels**.

As soon as the figure spotted the mouselings, he scampered off down a side street.

Instinctively, the Thea Sisters **QUICKENED** their pace.

When they reached the **ROLLING** metal gate in front of the pizzeria, Paulina gasped. "Look, everyone!" she exclaimed.

A *message* was

scrawled in dripping red paint on the gate:

BEWARE: THE FIRE DOES NOT FORGET —PHOENIX

Then Violet spotted the small cart, left behind by the dark figure. She **opened** the lid. Inside, there were cans of red paint.

Pamela studied the writing on the metal gate, shivering. Was this a threat? And who or what was Phoenix?

CLUE!

Why did the mysterious mouse write this note on the metal gate?

PHOENIX, AGAIN!

Pamela's heart was **BEATING** a mile a minute. She **scrambled** up the stairs of the house like a mouse just sprung from a glue trap! She needed to tell her father what had happened!

PJ looked up as Pam scampered into the room. But when she blurted out her news, he didn't seem surprised.

"We were expecting something like this," PJ sighed, **shaking** his head. "I'm afraid it's not the first message we've received."

Pamela could hardly believe her ears.

"I'm sorry, **Sweetie**," her dad continued as he placed his paw around her shoulder. "I didn't want to tell you because I didn't want to ruin your time here, but we received this letter a few days ago."

Pamela took the crumpled paper he handed her, and read it together with the THEA SISTERS. It said, Leave tribeca or your pizzas won't be the only things getting burned! —Phoenix

Pam's brother Vince explained, "Phoenix

LEAVE TRIBECA OR YOUR PIZZAS WON'T BE THE ONLY THINGS GETTING BURNED!

PHOENIX

has been trying to intimidate all of the store owners in **TRIBECA** by leaving these **THREATENING** notes. Now everyone is afraid he will set **FIRE** to their places. So far, Phoenix always acts at **NIGHT**, and no one has been able to figure out who he is."

Pam jumped to her paws. "We have to tell the **POLICE**!" she cried.

THE PHOENIX

The phoenix is a mythical bird from ancient Egyptian mythology. According to legend, each phoenix lives for five hundred to a thousand years. At the end of its life, a phoenix builds a nest and then sets itself and the nest on fire. The phoenix turns into ashes, from which a new phoenix is born.

She was so upset her whiskers trembled. Just then Grandpa Albie shuffled out of his bedroom in his pajamas and slippers. "Sounds like you've heard the news about **PHOENIX**," he sighed. "Too bad the **COPS** haven't had any luck catching him."

A minute later Mama Gianna joined the group in the living room, wrapping her **bathrobe** around her. Next Jo and Bella came out of their bedrooms. Soon the whole family had assembled.

Papa Johnny continued to explain. "We went into **debt** to renovate the restaurant," he said. "And now with these threats we may be forced to close. Our customers are too afraid to eat here. Everyone is afraid of Phoenix!"

Spike was the kind of mouseling who always stood up to bullies. He STAMPED his paws angrily. "But we can't close, Dad. We can't let one **rodent** scare our family!" he insisted.

Before long the whole family began **squeaking** about what to do about Phoenix.

"Spike is right," Pam said, ruffling her brother's fur. "We can't be **INTIMIDATED** by a bully who calls himself Phoenix!"

"You can say that again!" the **THEA SISTERS** shouted together.

"We can't be intimidated by a bully who calls himself **PHOENIX**!" Bella, Jo, and Sam repeated, giggling.

Everyone laughed along with them.

"What is a **PHOENIX**, anyway?" Georgie asked. "Isn't it some kind of bird?"

Flo, always the teacher, nodded. "The phoenix is actually an **ancient** Egyptian mythological **bird**," she explained.

Spike snorted. "Well, that decides it. We can't be afraid of something that doesn't even exist!" he announced.

"Well said!" Pamela squeaked. Then she stuck out her paw.

"Gimme FIVE, Brother!" she giggled.

GIMME FIVE!

A WONDERFUL IDEA!

In a few minutes, the THEA SISTERS and Pam's entire family were giving each other high fives.

When they finished, Paulina cleared her throat.

"I hate to **curdle** your cheese puffs, but what will you do about money?" Paulina asked Pamela's parents. "If you don't find new customers, you'll have to close, right?"

Vince nodded. "You're right," he squeaked. "But I have an idea. In a few days, it will be

HALLOWEEN

This holiday originated in Europe among the ancient Celts. It's celebrated on October 31. In New York, there's a big parade along Sixth Avenue (also called the Avenue of the Americas). Every year, more than fifty thousand people in costume march in the parade.

HALLOWEEN. We could raise money by selling pizzas during the big Halloween parade. Plus, it would be good publicity for the restaurant."

Everyone agreed that selling pizzas at the parade was a **WONDERFUL** idea. Before long, everyone in the group was **SHOUTING** out ideas and suggestions. But of course no one could hear anything, since everyone was talking at once.

Violet's *calm*, gentle, determined voice managed to silence them: "Grandpa Chen always says, 'In silence, all are wise, but in noise, all are deaf.'"

Then she divided everyone into groups and assigned each group a project for the **HALLOWEEN** parade celebration. Assignments in hand, everyone finally went back to bed.

READY FOR THE BIG APPLE?

The next morning, the Thea Sisters woke up well rested and went down to the kitchen to have **breakfast**.

"Mmm, I love **pancakes**!" Nicky exclaimed. She covered her pancakes in delicious **MAPLE SYRUP**. When the Thea Sisters were finished, they helped Mama Gianna with the dishes. Then they went outside.

They split up as soon as they left the building. Nicky headed off to Central Park to train for the **MARATHON**. Pamela and Paulina planned on investigating the mystery of **PHOENIX**. And Colette and Violet went in search of materials to make their **HALLOWEEN** costumes.

Meanwhile, everyone back at the restaurant was already working steadily to prepare a special pizza for the **COSTUME** parade.

Before leaving, Pam and Paulina went to say hello to Papa Johnny. They found him with a big **round** mouse, who was waving his paws around and **squeaking** in a loud voice.

Pamela whispered to Paulina, "That's *Whiskers*."

Actually, his name was *Marty McWhiskers*, but everyone called him Whiskers for short. He owned a small real estate agency in the neighborhood. But unfortunately, business wasn't exactly **BOOMING**. In fact, it was just the opposite. As the friends listened, Whiskers began blowing his nose noisily into his handkerchief and complaining.

"Tribeca is such a model neighborhood. It's a wonderful place to raise a family and put down roots," he sobbed. "But now it's just going to the **rats**! This **PHOENIX** character is really causing problems!"

Whiskers hung his head and began sobbing like a NeWBoRN mouselet. **SOB! SOB!**

PAULINA wasn't sure why, but there was something about the big mouse she didn't trust.

Whiskers noticed her staring at him. He shot her a **HARD** look, then put his paw around PJ and turned his back. Whiskers continued to **WHiMPER** in a low, purposeful voice.

"Just think how great the pizzeria used to be before all this trouble with **PHOENIX**," he reminded Pam's dad. "You used to have LINES wrapped around the block. Every night was a packed house. And the weekends? **HOLEY CHEESE!** Remember those? Rodents would wait forever for a slice! Now everyone's **running** scared. But don't worry, friend. I won't let you go bankrupt. I'm ready to buy your place at any time. All you have to do is **squeak**."

PJ nodded gratefully. "I appreciate your offer, **Whiskers**," he said. "But my children and I have new plans for the pizzeria. I think we can make it work!"

The **SCOWL** on Whiskers's face made Pamela furious. She had never liked Marty McWhiskers. Besides being extremely nosy, he was also **PUSHY** and obnoxious. Plus, why would he care if her dad wanted to make the pizzeria a **success** again? Was he jealous?

"Since when have you two been **friends**?"

she asked her dad after Whiskers *scampered* off.

PJ explained that Whiskers had done a lot to try to save the neighborhood. Sure, he was a bit **nosy**, but he had a good *heart*.

"He's been helping anyone who has been threatened by this **PHOENIX** scoundrel. He even offers to buy their property. Isn't that *generous*? The price he offered me would be at least enough to cover our **DEBTS**. I can't say I haven't considered it," he sighed.

"But we're not going to consider it now, right, Dad?" Pam interjected. "We can't give up on our **PIZZERIA**! It's a family *tradition*!"

PJ's face lit up with a wide grin. "We won't give up without a fight!" he agreed.

Pamela hugged her father. Then she headed off with Paulina to find out more about the *mysterious* Phoenix.

ON THE STREETS
OF NEW YORK

While PAMELA and PAULINA were still at the pizzeria, *Nicky*, **Violet**, and *Colette* had already reached the subway station. They were planning on taking the train to CENTRAL PARK.

The subway station was a blur of **activity**. Serious rodents in suits and ties rushed past teenagers with skateboards under their arms. Young female rodents dressed in the latest fashions raced by parents with babies in sleek strollers.

"**WOW!** This place sure is busy!" commented Nicky as the friends watched the crowd **swirling** around them. Then

THE NEW YORK CITY SUBWAY

The New York City subway runs along about 656 miles of working track, with 468 stations. The first part of the subway opened on October 27, 1904. It is the fourth-busiest public rail system in the world. Only the Tokyo, Moscow, and Seoul mass transit systems are busier. If there's a green light outside a New York subway station, that means it's open twenty-four hours; otherwise the light is red.

THE STREETS OF MANHATTAN

On most of the island of Manhattan, the streets form a grid. There are twelve numbered avenues that run up and down the island, roughly from north to south and parallel to the Hudson River. Two hundred twenty streets run across the island, roughly from west to east, and are perpendicular to the river.

they hopped onto their train and were off.

When the friends reached a stop on *Fifth Avenue*, a famous street full of expensive stores, they got off the train. Nicky headed straight for CENTRAL PARK.

"Don't wait for me for lunch!" she called back. "Today I'm planning an extra-**LONG** training session!"

Violet and Colette watched her run off into the distance.

"Poor Nicky," Colette sighed. "What a shame she has to miss all this!" She pointed in the direction of the stores, then did a little DANCE. "Just look at those HATS! And those shoes! And, wait . . . hold your whiskers . . . how cute are those PURSES?" she squeaked, hardly able to contain her excitement.

Violet rolled her eyes.

She could barely keep up with her friend as Colette darted from store to store like a mouse in a pinball machine.

"Um, Colette, we're supposed to be shopping for **HALLOWEEN** costumes, right?" Violet muttered.

"Oh, of course, Violet," Colette agreed as she scurried off toward a huge building

with the words Tiffany & Co. over the entrance.

Tiffany & Co. is a world-famous jewelry store that sells high-quality jewelry, crystal, and china. The windows of the store were full of SPARKLING necklaces, earrings, and rings. Violet watched Colette's head swivel around as she tried to take in all the sophisticated treasures.

"Isn't this place incredible, Violet?" Colette breathed, her eyes shining like the DIAMONDS in the glass case in front of her.

The store was impressive. But two hours later, even Colette was ready to go.

"The only problem with shopping on *Fifth Avenue* is that we can't buy anything," she said with a sigh. "It's all too EXPENSIVE!"

"Let's head back to TRIBECA to look for

our Halloween costumes," Violet suggested practically. "At least we won't go broke there!"

Colette agreed, and she and Violet headed to the subway for the ride back **downtown**.

PICK UP THOSE PAWS!

While Violet and Colette were window-shopping on Fifth Avenue, Nicky had arrived in **Central Park**. It was a beautiful fall day, and Nicky felt a **rush** of energy.

She headed for a path that ran along a body of water known as **the reservoir**.

CENTRAL PARK

Central Park was designed by landscape designers Frederick Law Olmsted and Calvert Vaux. The park first opened in 1859 and today covers 843 acres and is two and a half miles long and half a mile wide. Every day, thousands of New Yorkers and tourists visit the park to play sports, relax, work, and study. The park is equipped with many paths, playgrounds, playing fields, restaurants, a carousel, two ice-skating rinks, and a zoo.

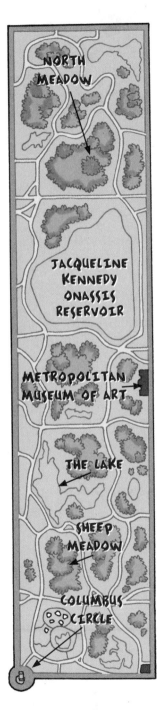

Nicky stopped to breathe in the fresh **air** and take in the sights. It was hard to believe she was still in **BUSTLING** New York City. Central Park was like a whole different world. There were green fields, lakes, fountains, and many **colorful** trees. Nicky watched the fall leaves **swirling** down from the trees. She was so happy. Who would ever have guessed that in only a few days, she would be competing in the **Big Apple Marathon**?

It was a **dream** come true!

She leaned against a post and **stretched** her leg muscles.

Around her, groups of young mouselings played in a field, a group of rodents were doing **yoga**, young professionals worked on their laptops, and others were simply enjoying the **sunshine**.

Nicky started her **STOPWATCH** and began to run, joining the many others who were making their way around the reservoir path.

Nicky's pace was **light** and easy. She felt relaxed and calm. A group of young female rodents had set up a picnic on a blanket nearby. Nicky smiled to herself. Maybe the **THEA SISTERS** could have a picnic in the park sometime.

But just then an angry voice interrupted her thoughts.

"Pick up those paws! *Faster! Faster!* CHEESE NIBLETS, your grandma Sluggyfur can run faster than that!"

Nicky slowed down to see who was making such a commotion, and practically got trampled over by another runner. When she looked up, she realized the mouse was none other than **Rhonda Razorpaws**! Her dad was coaching her from a **bicycle**. So that was whose voice Nicky had heard! Every five seconds, Mr. Razorpaws screamed another order at his daughter. HOW aNNOyiNg!

Nicky picked up her pace, hoping to catch up to **Rhonda**. After all, she couldn't let her rival beat her during their first meeting!

As soon as she caught up to Rhonda, Nicky greeted her with a friendly smile.

"**HI!**" Nicky squeaked as she scampered past her.

Rhonda's dad was furious. "Rhonda!" he shouted. "Don't let that little *fur ball* beat you! Get your **claws** out and leave her in the dust!"

Nicky couldn't believe her ears. What happened to good sportsmouseship? What kind of coaching advice was Rhonda's dad giving her?

At the next bend, Rhonda caught up to Nicky and passed her.

Nicky sped up again to rejoin her rival.

It was a race between Rhonda and Nicky, and it was a matter of pride.

AS SooN aS She caught up to her rival, Nicky greeted her with a friendly Smile as She passed her...

... but at the next bend, Rhonda joined Nicky and passed her...

Suddenly, Nicky realized that Rhonda wasn't doing it for her own pride, but out of **FEAR** of what her father would say if she slowed down. Nicky decided to **SLOW DOWN** and let Rhonda pass. Rhonda caught up to her father, a satisfied look on her snout.

"Good," he remarked. "But next time finish **FASTER**!"

. . . Nicky sped up again, to reach her rival . . .

. . . but then Nicky decided to slow down to let Rhonda pass.

TIME TO INVESTIGATE!

While Nicky was **RACING** around Central Park, Pamela and Paulina were racing around Tribeca, trying to discover the identity of **PHOENIX**. Their first stop was the local firehouse.

FIRE DEPARTMENT OF THE CITY OF NEW YORK (FDNY)

The first organized firefighting in New York City began in 1737 and was completely voluntary. After the Revolutionary War, the department was reorganized and named the Fire Department of the City of New York. Today the department consists of more than 11,400 officers and firefighters, 2,800 emergency medical technicians, and 1,200 civilian employees.

Pamela had an old friend who worked as a **firefighter**. "Maybe she can help us," Pam told Paulina.

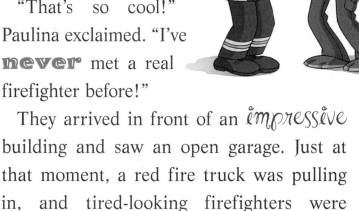

"That's so cool!" Paulina exclaimed. "I've **never** met a real firefighter before!"

They arrived in front of an *impressive* building and saw an open garage. Just at that moment, a red fire truck was pulling in, and tired-looking firefighters were getting off.

Pam approached one whose snout was dirty with **soot**.

"Excuse me, sir," she began *timidly*.

The firefighter burst out with a cheerful laugh: "**HA, HA, HA!**"

Then the rodent took off his helmet, and "he" turned into a she. Waves of curly copper hair fell to her shoulders. "Pamela, you haven't changed a bit! Don't you recognize me?" the mouse giggled. "It's me, Shirley!"

Pam blinked. "Shirley?" she squeaked. "I didn't recognize you with all of that soot on your snout." Pamela swiped her paw across Shirley's dirty fur.

"It's an OCCUPATIONAL HAZARD," Shirley said. "I had to go down a chimney to save a pet bird that was trapped. Rescuing pets is my SPECIALTY!"

"Rescuing a certain classmate who hadn't done her homework was also your specialty!" Pam cried, wrapping her friend in a warm hug.

"It's so FABUMOUSE to see you again,

Shirley!" Pamela said. "This is my friend Paulina. She studies at **MOUSEFORD ACADEMY** with me."

"It's a pleasure to meet you, Paulina," Shirley said, shaking her paw. "Now just give me five minutes. I'll clean up and then we can go *grab* some lunch."

COMPUTER WHiZ!

Shirley took the mouselings to a nearby restaurant.

"They make the best **sandwiches** here," she said, licking her whiskers in **anticipation**. Everyone laughed.

At the restaurant, the waiters greeted Shirley with friendly **smiles**.

In fact, everyone in the neighborhood knew Shirley well. She was outgoing, friendly, patient, and kind. And she was especially respected for her courageous work as a firefighter.

As soon as Pam described the threats from PHOENIX, Shirley's smile vanished. "I am so tired of hearing about that coward!" she exclaimed. "He even sent a THREATENING note to the fire station!"

Pamela couldn't believe Shirley had heard from Phoenix, too.

"I won't go back to Mouseford until I solve this mystery," she told Shirley. "I can't leave my family if they're in DANGER!"

Shirley nodded thoughtfully. "I have an idea," she told Pamela and Paulina. "We firefighters always write up detailed reports on every incident. They're all part of our **records**. Maybe we can compare all the different reports."

Pam and Paulina exchanged hopeful glances.

"You're amazing, Shirley!" Pam said as she gave her friend a big hug. "With your help, we'll solve this **Mystery**. I'm sure of it!"

After lunch, the mouselings returned to the station. Shirley took Pam and Paulina into an office filled with tons of equipment and **COMPUTERS**.

"From here we can connect to the central archives," Shirley explained, and started to punch in letters and numbers on the **KEYBOARD**. "Here's the data on all fire threats in the neighborhood. Maybe this will help you with the case."

Paulina looked closely at the screen. "Perhaps the dates and locations of the fire

threats are **connected**," she suggested. "Can I check?"

Shirley gave her seat to Paulina, whose paws began FLYING over the keyboard.

TAP–TAP–TAP–TAP–TAP–TAP–TAP–TAP–TAP–TAP

"**WOW!**" Shirley exclaimed with admiration. "You're a real **whiz** with COMPUTERS!"

Suddenly, a detailed **MAP** of Tribeca appeared on the screen, with a **RED** dot indicating the location of each fire threat that had been reported.

"**Holey cheesy burritos!**" Pamela exclaimed. "Do you see what I see?"

CLUE!

Papa Johnny's Pizzeria

What did Pamela notice about the map?

IT'S A DEAL!

While Pamela and Paulina were checking out the records at the fire station, Violet and Colette were checking out **HALLOWEEN** costumes back in Tribeca.

"Okay, *Colette*, let's see if we can actually buy something and not waste time window-shopping," Violet said in a gently **scolding** tone.

Colette was about to respond, but then she spotted a large **SALE** sign in front of a small fabric store. The friends went inside and were greeted warmly by an older rodent behind the counter.

"**WELCOME!**" she said. "Can I help you?"

"I hope so," Colette replied. "We need to create costumes for **HALLOWEEN**."

"I'm sorry, I don't have much left," the rodent replied. "But feel free to look around. Maybe you'll find something you can use."

Violet looked around. The shelves were half empty, but she noticed some bolts of bright-colored fabric **CRAMMED** into a corner. She also saw boxes of ribbons, buttons, spools of thread, and trimmings *SCATTERED* across the counter.

Colette examined the fabrics closely. "These are perfect!" she exclaimed. "Look at these **COLORS**, Violet!"

"If you take all of them, I can give you a special price," the rodent offered. "And I'll throw in some *ribbons*, too!"

"It's a deal!" Violet agreed without hesitation.

Colette picked up the fabric, then turned back to the older rodent. "These fabrics are beautiful," she said. "Can I ask you why you're selling off all of your merchandise?"

The older rodent shook her head sadly. "Oh, I'm afraid we've hit hard times and I've been forced to close," she said, folding the fabrics with care.

Violet and Colette looked at each other, concerned. Another store was closing? Did this have something to do with PHOENIX?

The rodent sighed.

"Recently we've received threats from someone called PHOENIX. Customers are AFRAID to come here now, and I'm AFRAID, too. So I've decided to move to

Kansas to live with my son," she said.

"And the store?!" Violet asked, shocked.

"I've sold it to **Marty McWhiskers**," the old mouse continued. "Thank goodness for him. He's the owner of the only realty agency in this area. He's offered to pay off my loan from the bank, so I agreed."

Colette and Violet shared a **look**.

They left the shop **WEIGHED** down with heavy packages and **HEAVIER** hearts.

> So the pizzeria wasn't the only place in trouble! The fabric store had also been threatened by Phoenix!

WHAT'S GOING ON?

Later that afternoon, Nicky arrived back at Pam's home to find the other Thea Sisters and some of Pam's family **DEEP** in conversation in the living room.

"What's going on?" *Nicky* asked curiously.

"We were just discussing the situation," Pam said.

"What situation?" Nicky asked.

"This one!" Paulina responded, pointing to a piece of paper on the table that showed a map of **TRIBECA**.

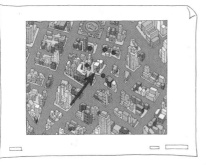

It had some **red dots** and a long **BLUE ARROW** on it.

"Pam's friend Shirley told us that the red dots are all of the places that have received **FIRE** threats in the last two years," Paulina explained.

"And this blue arrow?" Nicky asked.

"It's the fabric store where we bought materials for our **HALLOWEEN** costumes," Colette replied.

"We learned that the owner sold her shop to *Marty McWhiskers*," Violet explained.

Pam's dad chewed his whiskers, deep in

thought. "That's not the first time Whiskers has offered to help out," he mused.

Paulina nodded. "That's what doesn't seem right. Whiskers acts like a good neighbor, but maybe there's another reason that he's buying up all the real estate in Tribeca."

PAMELA handed her father a piece of paper. "These are the telephone numbers of all the rodents who have received THREATS from PHOENIX. Maybe if you call them, Dad, you'll find out if Whiskers has been offering to buy their properties, too."

PJ studied the list. Many of them were old friends who had since moved far away from Tribeca. One by one, Pam's dad called each number. When he hung up for the last time, he looked even more UPSET than when he'd begun dialing.

Pam put her paw on her dad's shoulder.

"I'm afraid it's just what we FEARED, honey," he confirmed. "All of these shop owners were threatened by PHOENIX, and Whiskers's agency bought each one out."

Vince began to walk BACK and FORTH across the room. "What a SCOUNDREL!" he squeaked. "He's trying to take over the entire block with his fake tears! Who could have imagined that he had enough money to buy all of these buildings?"

"It's easy to buy a shop when the owner is feeling desperate," Bella said sadly.

"Exactly!" Pam exclaimed. "The owner would feel lucky to get any offer at all!"

The THEA SISTERS shot each other knowing glances.

"Are you thinking what I'm thinking?" Pamela asked her friends.

"You bet we are!" Colette **exclaimed**. "Whiskers must be working with **PHOENIX**!"

"Or they're the **same** rodent!" Violet chimed in. "By **NIGHT** Phoenix writes threats on the stores' metal doors, and by day Whiskers **generously** offers to buy those same stores at rock-bottom prices!"

PJ nodded slowly. "But our suspicions aren't enough to expose Whiskers," he **WARNED**. "We need CONCRETE proof to take to the **POLICE**."

Nicky **twirled** her tail slowly. "If we

want to find proof, I think it's time we pay a visit to Whiskers's agency," she said.

Pamela **smiled**. "It looks like **HALLOWEEN** has arrived at just the right time," she announced with a mischievous grin. "We can go undercover!"

WHAT'S THE SITUATION SO FAR?

HERE ARE THE CLUES:

1) A mysterious character named Phoenix is threatening Pam's family and their pizzeria.

2) Phoenix writes messages with red paint on the metal doors of shops.

3) Many shops have been threatened by Phoenix, forcing the owners to leave the neighborhood.

4) Whiskers, the owner of a small real estate agency, always offers to help Phoenix's victims.

5) Pamela and Paulina discovered that the shops and buildings under threat were bought by Whiskers's agency.

LET'S GET READY!

The next day everyone began preparing for the upcoming **HALLOWEEN** parade.

Grandpa Albie was in charge of making sure everything ran smoothly.

He went from rodent to rodent, testing the delivery scooters, **listening** to music, and of course, sampling the special **pizzas**.

Pamela and Sam spent several hours in the garage. The expert **mechanics**

Pamela and Sam worked on the fabulous scooters . . .

... Violet and Nicky practiced their best musical pieces ...

worked on the scooters that would be used to sell pizzas during the *parade*.

Violet and Nicky practiced their best *musical* pieces so that they could draw people to the pizzeria with their singing.

Gus and Peggy, with Bella's help, designed flyers and then made fun masks with lots of different materials: feathers, **glitter**, beads, and SILVER thread. The mice selling pizza

... Gus, Peggy, and Bella made fun masks ...

would wear the masks to get into the **HALLOWEEN** spirit!

Paulina, Georgie, Colette, Jo, and Flo made **costumes** for everyone with the *ribbons* and fabrics Colette and Violet had bought at the **FABRIC** store.

Vince, Spike, PJ, and Mama Gianna made pizza after pizza . . . and Grandpa Albie happily approved them all!

When Halloween arrived, everything was finally ready. Pam's whole family looked

. . . and Vince, Spike, Papa Johnny, and Mama Gianna made pizza after pizza!

absolutely **FABUMOUSE** in their costumes.

Papa Johnny, Mama Gianna, Grandpa Albie, and the twins were dressed as **GHOSTS**. Vince was dressed as a skeleton. Flo, Bella, Spike, and Jo were all dressed as **VAMPIRES**. Sam was a **MONSTER**, and Georgie was dressed as a **pumpkin**.

Each of the Thea Sisters wore a costume, too.

Violet was a **VAMPIRE**. Colette was probably the first **PIRATE** ever to wear **lace** and a **heart-shaped** eye patch! Paulina made a darling **SCARECROW**. Nicky was rolled up in white bandages like a **MUMMY**. And Pamela was dressed as a **witch**.

Everyone was ready for the Halloween **PARADE** . . . and ready to unmask **PHOENIX**!

TRICK OR TREAT?

The **HALLOWEEN** parade started in Greenwich Village around seven o'clock, but the streets of **MANHATTAN** were filled with rodents in costumes by early afternoon.

Groups of COSTUMED mouselings knocked on the doors of houses and stores, asking, "**TRICK OR TREAT?!**"

Then they squealed with delight as the older rodents filled their bags with candy and other treats.

The pizzeria's decked-out **scooters** *SPED* back and forth through Tribeca, delivering freshly baked pizzas HOT from the oven. Pam's family was thrilled. Vince's idea was a huge success!

Meanwhile, the THEA SISTERS got ready for Operation Phoenix.

They scampered over to Whiskers's agency. Together, Pam, Violet, Paulina, Nicky, and Colette knocked on the door.

KNOCK! KNOCK!

Whiskers opened the door, surprised to see older mice trick-or-treating.

"**TRICK OR TREAT?!**" the friends squeaked, holding open their candy bags.

Whiskers scratched his head. "Aren't you five a little **old** for trick-or-treating?" he snickered.

The **THEA SISTERS** just smiled.

"Oh, you're never too old for **CANDY**," Colette said with a wide grin.

"Sure!" Nicky agreed. "It's not just for **mouselets**!"

"Don't you just love **HALLOWEEN**?" Pamela sighed.

OPERATION PHOENIX

When **Whiskers** took a few steps back into his office, the Thea Sisters followed him.

"Well, I'm afraid I don't have any **CANDY** to give you," the big mouse muttered. "I wasn't really expecting any **TRICK-OR-TREATERS** at the office."

"You really should have **CANDY** on Halloween," Colette scolded him. "It may help you attract clients. Plus, we passed a whole crowd of mouselings in costumes headed this way. They'll be **POUNDING** on your door at any minute."

Violet grabbed Whiskers's paw. "I have an idea," she said. "Why don't you go down to the corner store and buy a couple of bags of **CANDY**? We'll stay here and watch your place for you."

Whiskers smiled nervously at the mouselings. "Well, I guess maybe you're right," he agreed.

At that moment, Pam's brothers Sam and Georgie, pretending to be trick-or-treaters, arrived at the real estate agent's shop. They held out their bags and **GROWLED**, "Trick or treat! Trick or treat!"

"Better get that candy," Nicky advised Whiskers, shoving him gently out the door.

After Whiskers had left, Sam and Georgie stood guard at the door while the Thea Sisters **searched** the office.

Nicky and Colette **RUMMAGED** through the desk drawers.

Violet **inspected** the file cabinet.

Paulina *checked out* the computer.

And Pamela **opened** the closet.

"Cheese niblets!" she cried. In the closet

there was a staircase that led into a basement!

The mouselings followed each other down the stairs. It was so **DARK** they could hardly see!

Then they found a **light** switch and turned it on.

A huge room **appeared** in front of them. The walls were covered with maps, `newspaper clippings`, and photos of New York.

Paulina looked closer at one of the maps. "Look!" she squeaked. "It's marked with all the spots where Phoenix threatened to set **FIRES!**"

"Look at this!" Pamela said, pointing to a table. Sitting on top was a model of the Tribeca neighborhood. A gigantic structure made of steel and glass rose from the middle of the model. A **sign** at the top read **MCWHISKERS MEGA MALL.**

The building rose from the area that was currently occupied by Pam's family's **pizzeria** and the buildings Whiskers had forced out of business.

So his plan was to buy the stores in the neighborhood at low prices and then build a mall!

"What a scoundrel!" Pamela exclaimed.

"What a **crook**!" the others cried.

"Here's the evidence we've been looking for!" Paulina exclaimed, **PHOTOGRAPHING** the model and the map with her cell phone.

But PAMELA wasn't satisfied. "The deeds for the buildings *Whiskers* bought must

McWhiskers
Mega Mall

be around here somewhere," she insisted.

Pam started to **RUMMAGE** around again, but instead of finding documents, she found a garbage collector's uniform splattered with **RED** paint and a stamp bearing the symbol of a phoenix.

Here was the final evidence: *Whiskers* and **PHOENIX** had to be the SAME MOUSE!

CLUE!

The fake garbage collector had been Whiskers in disguise ...

... and he was also the one who had stamped the notes with the symbol belonging to Phoenix!

 These were the final clues the Thea Sisters needed! The fake garbage collector had been Whiskers in disguise, and he was also the one who had stamped the notes with the symbol belonging to Phoenix!

An Escape!

The Thea Sisters went back UPSTAIRS.

Just then Whiskers stumbled through the front door with a shopping bag filled with CANDY.

"Wh-wh-what's going on?" he stammered.

The THEA SISTERS stuck the evidence they'd found in the BASEMENT under Whiskers's nose.

"What does this mean?" Pam asked, showing him the garbage collector's uniform.

"And this?" Paulina added, holding up Phoenix's red stamp.

Whiskers blinked and his face turned **red**. "Um, w-well, it's not what you think," he stammered.

But instead of explaining, Whiskers pushed

Pamela aside, throwing her against her brothers Georgie and Sam. Then he grabbed Violet's black **cape**, put it over his shoulders, and **SCAMPERED** away!

"DON'T LET HIM ESCAPE!"

Pamela squeaked, taking off after him.

The Thea Sisters **THREW** themselves into the chase.

They almost caught up to him. But unfortunately they arrived in the SoHo neighborhood just as the **HALLOWEEN** parade was passing by. In a second, the five mice lost Whiskers. In the middle of the mass of rodents in cos†umes and parade **FL°ATS**, it was impossible for the Thea Sisters to find him.

"What **ROTTEN** luck!" Paulina cried, pushing her way through the crowd. "I can't see him anymore!"

"We've lost him." Violet sighed.

But Pamela wasn't ready to give up. With a determined squeak, she climbed up the first float that passed by. At the top, Pam peered down at the paradegoers rushing by on the street.

"There he is!" she shouted a second later. "I see him! He's headed for Houston Street!"

Answer:
Whiskers is in box H-6.

The Thea Sisters **scampered** after him, but **Whiskers** made a mad **dash** down a side street and into an open parking garage.

What luck! He found a **CAR** with the keys left in the ignition! The THEA SISTERS got there just in time to watch Whiskers **speed** out of the lot.

"We'll never get him now!" Colette **moaned**.

But just then a fire truck with a familiar driver showed up.

"Shirley!" Pamela shouted, recognizing her friend. "Whiskers stole that car and we have to **catch** him!" she cried, pointing out the car that was **screeching** away ahead of them. "Will you help us?"

"Of course I'll help," Shirley replied. "But who is **Whiskers**?"

"We'll explain later!" Pam squeaked. "But we have to get going—he's getting **away**!" Shirley **sprang** into action. She quickly helped the Thea Sisters onto the truck and turned on the truck's **SIREN**.

"Buckle your seat belts and hold on **TIGHT**!" Shirley **yelled** to the group.

THE CHASE!

Whiskers sped through the streets of **NEW YORK**, avoiding the parade as he **careened** down the city's back alleyways.

The wheels of the car skidded and **SCREECHED**. Whiskers took the narrowest streets, trying hard to lose the fire truck.

VROOOOOOM!

skreeech!!!

Every time the **THEA SISTERS** thought they had caught up, **Whiskers** managed to slip away.

But Shirley wasn't going to give up!

She knew the streets of **MANHATTAN** like the back of her **paw**, and she was able to anticipate Whiskers's every move.

If he thought he could cleverly lose them in

HOTEL

MC72R6

vrrooommm!!!

a street that was too NARROW for the truck, Shirley would be waiting for him on the other side.

She stuck to him like mozzarella MELTING on a pizza!

They went down a long, straight street. The two vehicles were so close they were almost touching!

"FASTER, Shirley, we're almost there!" Pamela shouted.

"I can't pass him," Shirley replied. "The street isn't wide enough!"

Then Nicky had an idea. "Let's extend the fire truck's LADDER and jump onto the CAR!"

Shirley looked at Nicky for a moment.

"It's very dangerous. . . . Do you really think you can do it?!"

Nicky smiled. Then she threw open one

of the truck's windows and climbed up on top. With every JOLT of the truck, Nicky risked losing her grip, but she managed to *hang* on tight. Finally, she reached the **LADDER**.

"Release the ladder, Shirley!" Nicky shouted at the top of her lungs.

A nerve-wracking moment passed, and then, with a metallic noise, the long ladder began to *move*.

THE END OF
THE ROAD

Nicky clung tightly to the **LADDER**, which was now extended all the way. Whiskers was right underneath her.

Nicky looked ahead and realized the **ROAD** was coming to an end. Soon they would be right on **BROADWAY**, the main avenue in Manhattan. It would be impossible to carry out Nicky's plan once they hit that busy street!

If she didn't **JUMP** now, it would be too late!

Nicky pushed off and leaped.

She fell with a **THUMP** into the backseat.

Whiskers hit the brakes.

SCREEEEEEEEEEEEEEEEEEEEEEEEEEECH

The car skidded to a stop between two **garbage** bins. Nicky jumped out of the backseat and flung herself at Whiskers.

"There's no way out!" she shouted, taking hold of his shoulders with a **judo** grip.

Shirley and the other Thea Sisters rushed to help Nicky.

Whiskers had been caught!

"You little **BRATS**!" he squeaked. "You ruined everything! I was one pawstep away from having my dreams come true."

"You should feel *ASHAMED* of yourself!" Pamela scolded him. "Think of all the good rodents you forced to leave TRIBECA by scaring them with your threats!"

"Oh, who cares about them?" Whiskers said with a SCOWL. "They'll be better off anyway. I was going to build the **BIGGEST**, the greatest, the most beautiful mall in New York! It would have been **spectacular**! All I had to do was get rid of that **ROTTEN** pizzeria!"

"You mean my dad's **Restaurant**!" Pamela fumed. Meanwhile, Shirley tied Whiskers's paws tightly together.

"I'm sure the **POLICE** will be happy to hear your confession!" Paulina said.

Whiskers **groaned**. Shirley put in a call to the local police station, and a few minutes later they arrived to cart Whiskers off to **jail**.

"Bye-bye, **PHOENIX**!" Shirley and the Thea Sisters called after him, grinning.

LET'S PARTY!

The **THEA SISTERS** returned to Whiskers's real estate agency to pick up Sam and Georgie. Then they drove to the **POLICE** station to make sure *Whiskers* was locked up **TIGHT**.

Later that evening they returned to the **HALLOWEEN** celebration, which was still going on in the streets.

"**LET'S PARTY!**" Nicky and Colette said as they headed for the cheery crowd of costumed rodents.

The Thea Sisters sang, danced, and threw confetti and *streamers* along with the other rodents in the crowd. Pamela was so happy they had captured Phoenix her grin *STRETCHED* from ear to ear.

"Hooray for Tribeca! Hooray for **Papa Johnny's Pizzeria**!" she shouted.

The Thea Sisters joined in clapping and cheering, "**HOORAY! HOORAY! HOORAY!**"

But the night's surprises weren't over yet.

Back in **TRIBECA**, the **THEA SISTERS** discovered that the performance organized by Flo, Jo, and Spike had **transformed** into a real **dance** competition, with break dancing and hip-hop music.

Lots of other rodents had joined them.

Nicky and Violet grabbed their guitar and violin and filled the night air with beautiful music.

Paulina and Colette **enthusiastically** joined the dancing.

But the real **queen** of the party was Pamela. She, Spike, Sam, and Georgie

performed a DiZZYiNG series of **hip-hop** dance moves that wowed the crowd.

A **witch**, a MONSTER, a **pumpkin**, and a VAMPIRE... what a show!

IT'S A SECRET!

The next day the THEA SISTERS decided to spend the whole day relaxing. While the friends rested, Pam's family held a secret meeting. The day of the **Big Apple Marathon** was drawing near. They wanted to do something special for Nicky. So they decided to organize a special CHEERING section just for her.

They called all their friends and relatives. They asked them if they would help cheer from the sidelines. Grandpa Albie even called some friends from the bowling league he used to play in. Everyone agreed to help.

Meanwhile, Pam's sisters were busy, too.

"What are you up to?" Paulina asked when

she passed by their bedroom. Flo, Jo, and Bella grinned.

"We're making some BANNERS to give to our friends along the route of the **Marathon**. That way Nicky will always

feel our support," they explained. "But don't tell her. It's a **secret**!"

"That's so **sweet**!" Paulina exclaimed. "And don't worry. These lips are **ZIPPED**. Plus, I've just had another great idea! We can film Nicky's whole race with video cameras and cell phones and I can send the images back to **MOUSEFORD** live! That way even the rodents at the academy can **cheer** for her!"

THREE, TWO, ONE . . . GO!

Finally, the day they'd been waiting for arrived.

The **THEA SISTERS** accompanied Nicky to the starting line and quickly lost sight of her in the crowd of participating athletes.

Shirley, though, as a **FIREFIGHTER**, had found them a unique spot to watch the start: a cherry picker, which is a special platform attached to a super-**TALL** ladder.

"Come on, Nicky!" the mice shouted.

The front of the starting line was reserved for the fastest runners. While Nicky was in the middle of more than thirty thousand participants, **Rhonda Razorpaws** had managed to get a spot much closer to the front.

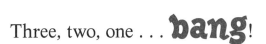

Three, two, one . . . **bang**!

The athletes at the front of the race began running, followed by the other athletes. Everyone was **JAMMED** together in one big crowd, each trying to find enough room to quicken his or her pace. After about half a mile, the ЅNAKе of athletes had lengthened, leaving each runner with his or her own space.

Nicky was super-focused: "I mustn't push myself too hard!" she repeated. "I mustn't **BURN** all my energy right away, since I'll need it later!"

Nicky was surprised by the loud cheers of the crowd. She couldn't believe it when she heard her own name shouted through a megaphone: "**Nɪ-CKY! Nɪ-CKY! Nɪ-CKY!**"

GO, NiCKY!

Nicky spotted Georgie, Flo, and Jo in the crowd, waving their paws so that she could find them. Above them, a fluttering banner read GO, NICKY!

Just then she felt a sudden burst of ENERGY. It was as if she had wings on her feet! Carefully, she began to pass other runners one by one. And then, right in front of her, she spotted a blue jersey with a silver crest on it. It was the symbol of **RATRIDGE ACADEMY**. "Rhonda!" Nicky said to herself as she picked up her pace.

Nicky controlled her speed so that she could keep Rhonda at just the right distance in front of her.

At this pace, the miles passed by QUICKLY.

Finally, Nicky saw a sign that indicated that she had about ten miles to go. As the road began a slight incline, she remembered reading somewhere that the last few miles of the course were full of hills.

OH, NO! she thought. Suddenly, just thinking about the UPS AND DOWNS she would have to face at the very end made her feet feel heavier than blocks of **lead**. She was getting tired earlier than she had expected, and that *worried* her. How would she find the strength to get all the way to the finish line?!

Nicky saw a rest stop along the route.

She ran up to it and took a cup of **water**.

Even Rhonda paused at the rest stop to get a **drink**. And when she looked around, she saw Nicky right behind her!

It was exactly at this moment that I

spotted Nicky on the television screen from the Mouseford school lounge.

"GO, MOUSEFORD!" I shouted, as though Nicky could hear me. And who knew? Maybe somewhere deep in her heart she could feel my love and support!

Back in New York City, the runners had reached the final stretch.

Nicky noticed that Rhonda had started to **SLOW** down. It was the perfect chance to pass her.

Nicky spotted another banner that read **GO, NICKY!!!**

She got ready to pass her rival. But just then, her foot landed on a **wet** sponge.

OOPS!

SQUISH!

HEAD-TO-HEAD!

Nicky slipped and felt a sharp pain in her ankle.

Her **HEART** beat wildly. *No! Not an accident! she thought. Not now! Not during the* **Marathon**!

She started to run again, this time a bit more slowly. Her ankle **THROBBED**, but it was just twisted. If she kept running and kept *moving*, she just might make it!

Rhonda, on the other paw, was starting to pull ahead again.

While Nicky was trying to catch up to Rhonda, Grandpa Albie and his friends were cheering for the lead runners near the **FINISH LINE** at the entrance to Central Park.

The **winner**—a male mouse who

finished the race in two hours and eight minutes—arrived. Then the first female rodent crossed the finish line at two hours and twenty minutes.

The **ATHLETES** were tired but joyful.

After another hour, Grandpa Albie spotted Nicky in the crowd of runners who were just reaching **CENTRAL PARK**. As soon as he saw her, Grandpa started up a wild concert of whistles and noisemakers.

WHOO-WHOOO! WHEEEET!

Grandpa Albie waved the Mouseford flag and shouted, "Go, Nicky! Let those paws fly!"

Nicky was speechless at the sight of all the rodents who had come just for her. How could she **DISAPPOINT** all her enthusiastic supporters? There was only a little farther to go. It was time for one last burst of energy!

Nicky spotted Rhonda right in front of her again. Her pace was **LABORED** and she was trying to elbow her way past an athlete next to her. What an unsportsmouselike move!

But Rhonda had her work cut out for her: The athlete moved away at the last second, Rhonda lost her balance, and she landed with her paws in the .

"She had it coming!" Colette would have said, and Nicky felt a rush of amusement and wanted to laugh.

But then she felt sorry for Rhonda. Rhonda had made it this far, and it would be awful if she decided to quit now. Nicky ran to Rhonda and reached out a paw to help her up. Rhonda looked shocked as she whispered, "Thanks."

Nicky smiled and threw herself back into the race. Helping Rhonda had given her a surge of good feelings and renewed energy. And when she saw PAMELA, PAULINA, Violet, and Colette waving their paws in the middle of the crowd, she felt like she was flying over the finish line.

Yes, she'd made it!

She'd run her first marathon!

CONGRATULATIONS!

A few minutes later **Rhonda** crossed the finish line, too. She smiled *warmly* at Nicky. Then she walked up to her and shook her paw.

"Congratulations!" she said. "And thanks for helping me out back there. You really are a great *runner*. What's your secret?"

Nicky was about to respond when she was joined by the **THEA SISTERS**. They were followed by Pam's family and all their friends. Vince **LIFTED** Nicky onto his shoulders.

"Let's go to the pizzeria to **CELEBRATE!**" he shouted.

Nicky looked down and saw Rhonda walking away.

"I'll be back in just a minute," she told her friends.

Then she caught up with Rhonda.

"I don't have a secret when it comes to running, Rhonda," she said. "But I think what pushes me to do my best are my friends. Maybe we could be friends, too. Why don't you come celebrate with us?"

Rhonda glanced at her father, who was waiting nearby with a stern look. "I can't," she replied. "But thanks for inviting me, Nicky. You really are a special mouse."

PiZZA PARTY

Back at the family pizzeria, everyone was in high spirits. Not only had Nicky done a great job running the Big Apple Marathon, but the Thea Sisters had solved a *mystery* and the pizzeria had been saved.

"**Cheese niblets**, you mouselings have had quite an adventure this week," Mama Gianna exclaimed, giving Pamela a squeeze.

"We sure have!" the THEA SiSTERS squeaked at the exact same time, causing everyone to laugh.

"Now that's what I call **teamwork**!" chuckled Grandpa Albie.

While they were still celebrating, Paulina's cell phone rang.

It was Professor Octavius de Mousus at **MOUSEFORD ACADEMY**. He asked to speak to Nicky.

"My dear Nicky!" the professor boomed when Nicky got on the phone. "Congratulations on beating the athlete from Ratridge! But it's even more wonderful that you gave her a helping paw. Well done! Now I'm going to pass the phone to someone who wants to say hello!"

Can you guess who it was? Well, it was me, THEA STILTON, of course.

I told Nicky how proud I was of her.

After Nicky hung up the phone, PJ asked everyone to go outside to see the new shop **SIGN**, which was still covered by a sheet.

"We've changed the name of the restaurant," he announced. "In honor of the THEA SISTERS, from now on the pizzeria will be called **FABUMOUSE FRIENDS PIZZERIA**!"

The **THEA SISTERS** thanked PJ. Then they hugged each other.

It was a truly **MARVELOUS** gift — almost as marvelous as their friendship!

Thea Sisters

Want to read the next adventure
of the Thea Sisters?
I can't wait to tell you all about it!

THEA STILTON AND THE ICE TREASURE

The Thea Sisters are invited to travel to Alaska for a conference held by the Green Mice, an important ecological association. Their host and his family are native Alaskans who welcome the five mice and make them feel at home in the snowy climate. But soon there's trouble: The Thea Sisters discover that someone is upsetting the ecosystem by blowing up the ice with explosives! Can the Thea Sisters stop the destruction and save the ice?

And don't miss any of my other fabumouse adventures!

THEA STILTON AND THE DRAGON'S CODE

THEA STILTON AND THE MOUNTAIN OF FIRE

THEA STILTON AND THE GHOST OF THE SHIPWRECK

THEA STILTON AND THE SECRET CITY

THEA STILTON AND THE MYSTERY IN PARIS

THEA STILTON AND THE CHERRY BLOSSOM ADVENTURE

THEA STILTON AND THE STAR CASTAWAYS

Want to read my next adventure?
I can't wait to tell you all about it!

RUN FOR THE HILLS, GERONIMO!

I, Geronimo Stilton, was about to leave on a relaxing vacation all by myself. I was planning to kick back and connect with nature in the beautiful Black Hills of South Dakota. But somehow, my peaceful trip quickly turned into a crazy treasure hunt — with the entire Stilton family in tow! Our journey even included a hot-air-balloon ride over Mount Rushmore. Holey cheese! Have I mentioned that I'm afraid of heights? This was one adventure I'd never forget!

And don't miss any of my other fabumouse adventures!

#1 Lost Treasure of the Emerald Eye

#2 The Curse of the Cheese Pyramid

#3 Cat and Mouse in a Haunted House

#4 I'm Too Fond of My Fur!

#5 Four Mice Deep in the Jungle

#6 Paws Off, Cheddarface!

#7 Red Pizzas for a Blue Count

#8 Attack of the Bandit Cats

#9 A Fabumouse Vacation for Geronimo

#10 All Because of a Cup of Coffee

#11 It's Halloween, You 'Fraidy Mouse!

#12 Merry Christmas, Geronimo!

#13 The Phantom of the Subway

#14 The Temple of the Ruby of Fire

#15 The Mona Mousa Code

#16 A Cheese-Colored Camper

#17 Watch Your Whiskers, Stilton!

#18 Shipwreck on the Pirate Islands

**#19 My Name Is
Stilton, Geronimo
Stilton**

**#20 Surf's Up,
Geronimo!**

**#21 The Wild,
Wild West**

**#22 The Secret
of Cacklefur
Castle**

A Christmas Tale

**#23 Valentine's
Day Disaster**

**#24 Field Trip to
Niagara Falls**

**#25 The Search
for Sunken
Treasure**

**#26 The Mummy
with No Name**

**#27 The
Christmas Toy
Factory**

**#28 Wedding
Crasher**

**#29 Down and
Out Down Under**

**#30 The Mouse
Island Marathon**

**#31 The
Mysterious
Cheese Thief**

**Christmas
Catastrophe**

**#32 Valley of the
Giant Skeletons**

**#33 Geronimo
and the Gold
Medal Mystery**

**#34 Geronimo
Stilton, Secret
Agent**

**#35 A Very Merry
Christmas**

**#36 Geronimo's
Valentine**

#37 The Race
Across America

#38 A Fabumouse
School Adventure

#39 Singing
Sensation

#40 The Karate
Mouse

#41 Mighty
Mount
Kilimanjaro

#42 The Peculiar
Pumpkin Thief

#43 I'm Not a
Supermouse!

#44 The Giant
Diamond Robbery

#45 Save the
White Whale!

#46 The Haunted
Castle

And coming soon!

#47 Run for the Hills,
Geronimo!

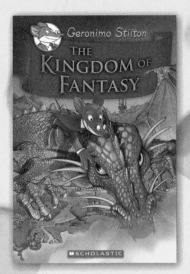

THE KINGDOM OF FANTASY

THE QUEST FOR PARADISE:
THE RETURN TO THE KINGDOM OF FANTASY

THE AMAZING VOYAGE:
THE THIRD ADVENTURE IN THE KINGDOM OF FANTASY

I, *Geronimo Stilton*, have a lot of
mouse friends, but none as **spooky**
as my friend CREEPELLA VON CACKLEFUR!
She is an enchanting and MYSTERIOUS
mouse with a pet bat named Bitewing.
YIKES! I'm a real 'fraidy mouse,
but even I think CREEPELLA and
her family are AWFULLY
fascinating. I can't wait
for you to read all
about CREEPELLA in these
fa-mouse-ly funny and
spectacularly spooky tales!

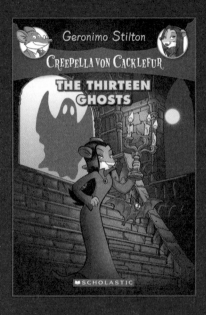

#1 THE THIRTEEN GHOSTS

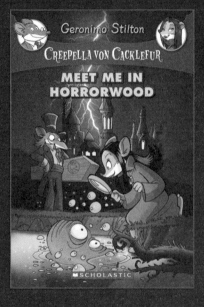

#2 MEET ME IN HORRORWOOD

THANKS FOR READING,
AND GOOD-BYE UNTIL OUR
NEXT ADVENTURE!

Thea Sisters